SPRINGTIME
FOR JEANNE~MARIE

by

Françoise

Charles Scribner's Sons   New York

Copyright 1955 by Charles Scribner's Sons   Printed in the United States of America

SBN684-12633-8   A–9.71[ML]

It is springtime.

The fields are green.

Jeanne-Marie and her pet sheep

Patapon

go to pick flowers.

Madelon the white duck goes too.

Jeanne-Marie sings a little song:

"Jeanne-Marie

Patapon

Madelon

We are three."

"Beh-beh-beh!" says Patapon.

"Quack-quack-quack!" says Madelon.

"Jeanne-Marie, we are three."

Every bright spring day
Jeanne-Marie and Patapon
take the white duck to the river.
It is a little river
that runs past the farm.
Madelon the white duck
swims on the river.
Jeanne-Marie and Patapon watch her.
"Swim, swim, Madelon,"
says Jeanne-Marie.
"But be sure to come back.
Don't go too far!"

Every day
Madelon swims on the river.
She does not go too far.
But one day . . .
Down the river goes Madelon,
far away
and out of sight.
And she does not come back!
"Beh-beh-beh!"
bleats Patapon.
"Madelon is gone!"

So Jeanne-Marie and
Patapon walk along the river
to find Madelon.
They meet the postman on his bicycle.
"Good-morning, Jeanne-Marie,
good-morning, Patapon,"
says the postman.
"Good-morning," says Jeanne-Marie.
"Have you seen
a little white duck named Madelon?"
"No," says the postman.
"I was so busy. I have not seen
a little white duck named
Madelon."

So Jeanne-Marie and
Patapon walk along the river
to find Madelon.
They come to the school.
All the children are coming out.
"Have you seen a little white duck?"
asks Jeanne-Marie.
"A little white duck named Madelon?"
"No," says Marie.
"No," says Michel.
"No," says Lisette.
"No, we have not seen
a little white duck named
Madelon."

So Jeanne-Marie and
Patapon walk along the river
to find Madelon.
They see a young man fishing.
"Good morning," says Jeanne-Marie.
"Have you seen
a little white duck named Madelon?"
"What?" says the young man.
"Please don't make so much noise.
You will frighten the fish!
No, I have not seen
a little white duck named
Madelon."

Jeanne-Marie and
Patapon go along the river
very slowly.
They are sad — so sad.
"Patapon," says Jeanne-Marie,
"Maybe we will never
find Madelon.
Maybe she has gone
all the way to the sea,
Patapon.
Maybe, maybe."

So Jeanne-Marie and
Patapon walk along the river
to find Madelon.
They meet a little boy in a boat.
"Oh!" says Jeanne-Marie,
"We have lost
our little white duck, Madelon.
We are so sad!"
"Do not be sad!" says the little boy.
"My name is Jean-Pierre.
Come into my boat.
I'll help you to find your white duck
Madelon."

So Jeanne-Marie
Patapon and Jean-Pierre
go along the river
to find Madelon.
And they ask everyone they meet:
"Have you seen
a little white duck named Madelon?"
And everyone answers

NO

And no- and no- and no.
No one has seen
Madelon.

Jeanne-Marie cries
and cries.
'Maybe Madelon is drowned!"
"No," says Jean-Pierre.
"Ducks never get drowned!
Don't you know that?
Look at that little farm.
It's my house
and we have five ducks.
Stop crying,
and I'll give you one.
Come on, Jeanne-Marie,
come on!"

It is such a charming farm,
with a small pond.
On the pond are . . .
what? . . . what?

6

white ducks, not five!
"Oh, Patapon," says Jeanne-Marie,
"Oh, Patapon, do you think. . . ."
"Beh-beh-beh," says Patapon.
"Maybe, maybe,
Jeanne-Marie."

So they all call:
"Madelon! Madelon! Madelon!"
And Madelon
the naughty white duck
comes swimming.
Jeanne-Marie picks her up.
"Quack, quack, quack!"
says Madelon.
"Quack, quack,
quack!"

"Oh!" says Jeanne-Marie.
"you naughty Madelon!
Now let us go home.
"Come, Madelon,
"come, Patapon.
Now we are all together again."
"Beh-beh-beh," says Patapon.
"Quack, quack, quack,"
says Madelon.
Home they go along the river.

Now, Jeanne-Marie
and Patapon and Madelon
have a friend.
Jeanne-Marie does not cry
any more.
She sings a little song:
"Jeanne-Marie,
Patapon,
Madelon,
We are three."
Jean-Pierre says,
"But what about me?"

"Beh-beh-beh," says Patapon.
"Quack-quack-quack,"
says Madelon.
"Now we are four!"